My DADDY is the BEST

 FIVE QUILLS

MY DADDY IS THE BEST

Mijn papa heeft een staart

First published in Belgium and the Netherlands in 2020

by Clavis Uitgeverij, Hasselt – Alkmaar – New York

Text and illustrations copyright © 2020

Clavis Uitgeverij, Hasselt – Alkmaar – New York

All rights reserved.

Published in 2021 by Five Quills

93 Oakwood Court, London W14 8JZ, Great Britain

www.fivequills.co.uk

Five Quills and associated logos are trademarks of Azura Press Ltd.

English text by Natascha Biebow at Blue Elephant Storyshaping

A CIP record for this title is available from the British Library

ISBN 978-1-912923-24-3

1 3 5 7 9 10 8 6 4 2

Printed in the EU by Pulsio Print

My DADDY is the BEST

Guido Van Genechten

 Five Quills

"Daddy, what's that strange green thing down there?"
Isabella asked one day.

"That's my tail," Daddy said proudly.

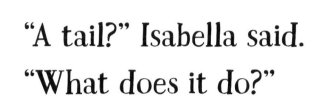

"A tail?" Isabella said.
"What does it do?"

"Watch," Daddy said. "I'll show you."

"Hold on to it, sailor!
We're going into the water!"

"Now, listen carefully," Daddy said.
"If you pull my tail to the right,
we'll go left."

"And if you pull my tail to the left . . ."

"We'll go right," Isabella said.

"YES!" Daddy said.

Isabella loved steering.

To the left.

To the right.

To the left.

To the right.

To the left.

right

To the left.

left

left

right

right

right

right

left

Straight ahead!

And Daddy was the best ship ever.

After sixty-six loops and six hours of sailing,
the ship ran out of fuel.

"Let's go and dry out in the sun," Daddy gasped.
"This is so nice . . . **Zzzzz** . . ."

Five minutes later, Isabella called out:
"Daddy, I'm all dry! Daddy? DADDY!
Wake up, sleepy tail!"

Daddy sleepily shook the mud off his scales. Oops!

"Oh yes . . ." Daddy said.
"There's something else
I can do with my tail.
A balancing trick. Look."

"Wowee!" Isabella said.

Now she was sure.

"I want a tail too!"
"A tail?" Daddy asked. "All right . . .
But are you very, very sure?"
Isabelle nodded. "Very, very, very sure."
"Then look behind you and you will see . . ."

" . . . your very own TAIL!"
"A tail! Daddy, look,
I have a tail just like YOU!"

Fun-filled picture books by Five Quills

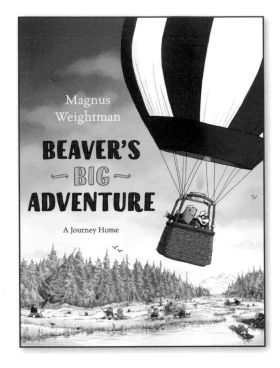

Magnus Weightman

BEAVER'S BIG ADVENTURE

A Journey Home

The Truth About **DINOSAURS**

Guido Van Genechten

The ~~Ferocious~~ **CHOCOLATE** Wolf

Lizzie Finlay

FIVE QUILLS

Visit us on www.fivequills.co.uk